Isla
the Ice Star
Fairy

Special thanks to
Narinder Dhami

ORCHARD BOOKS
338 Euston Road, London NW1 3BH
Orchard Books Australia
Level 17/207 Kent Street, Sydney, NSW 2000
A Paperback Original

First published in 2011 by Orchard Books

A CIP catalogue record for this book is available
from the British Library.

ISBN 978 1 40831 292 6

5 7 9 10 8 6

Printed in Great Britain

The paper and board used in this paperback are natural recyclable
products made from wood grown in sustainable forests. The
manufacturing processes conform to the environmental regulations
of the country of origin.

Orchard Books is a division of Hachette Children's Books,
an Hachette UK company.

www.hachette.co.uk

Isla
the Ice Star
Fairy

by Daisy Meadows

ORCHARD

Jack Frost's Ice Castle

Swan Theatre

THE SWAN THEATRE

Funky Feet Dance Studios

Tippington Ice Rink

Who likes talent shows? Not me!
So, goblins, listen carefully,
Each Showtime Fairy has a star,
Their magic glitters near and far.

Now do exactly as I say,
And steal these magical stars away,
Then, when our wicked work is done,
We can spoil all showtime fun!

Contents

Slipping and Sliding

"Only one day left before the Variety Show!" Kirsty exclaimed. She and Rachel were inside Tippington Ice Rink, gazing at the perfect, gleaming square of ice surrounded by rows of seats. "It's been *so* exciting watching all the auditions, hasn't it, Rachel?"

Rachel nodded. It was the half-term holiday and all local schools, including Rachel's, had been taking part in auditions for magic, drama, acrobatics, dance and singing. The best acts would be performing in the Tippington Variety Show at the end of the week. Everyone was hoping that the show would raise enough money to build an adventure playground, a bandstand and an outdoor theatre in the town's Oval Park. Now it was the final day of auditions, and a pair of ice-skaters would be chosen to take part in the show tomorrow.

"I'm really glad you're staying with me this week, Kirsty," Rachel said with a smile. "Having a wonderful fairy adventure just wouldn't be the same without *you*!"

On the very first day of the auditions the girls had been thrilled when the Showtime Fairies had asked for their help. The Showtime Fairies had extra-special magical stars fixed to the tips of their wands, and they used this powerful magic to make sure that everyone in both the human and the fairy worlds could develop their showtime talents to the full. But while the Showtime Fairies had been rehearsing for their own Variety Show, Jack Frost had been plotting and planning to ruin everything. He'd sent his goblins to steal the Showtime Fairies' magical stars and hide them away in the human world. Because of this, both humans and fairies had lost their showtime skills, but so far Rachel and Kirsty had helped the Showtime Fairies find five of their missing stars.

"And today we're looking for Isla the Ice Star Fairy's magical star," Kirsty pointed out, as she and Rachel sat down on a wooden bench to put on the skates they'd hired. "I hope we find it in time for the audition."

"I wonder if the goblins will be here today?"

Rachel remarked, lacing up her skates. Jack Frost's goblins had been turning up to the auditions, pretending they were from a school called Icy Towers. Jack Frost had no idea that the goblins planned to use the magic in the Showtime Fairies' stars to cheat and win all the auditions, instead of ruining them. But so far they hadn't succeeded, thanks to Rachel, Kirsty and the fairies.

"I'm *sure* they will," Kirsty replied. "After all, this is their last chance to use the Showtime Fairies' magic to make themselves into stars!" She glanced around the empty rink as she tied her laces tightly. "But they don't seem to be here at the moment. I'm glad we got here early, though, so we can keep an eye out for them!"

13

"And we'll be able to watch the auditions a little later, too," Rachel added. "My friends Kayla and Adam are skating for Tippington School."

"That'll be fun – *if* we find Isla's star before then." Kirsty stood up. "I can't wait to have a go myself. Come on, Rachel!" And Kirsty glided off confidently across the dazzling white ice. Rachel stood up too, but she was looking a bit nervous.

"I haven't skated since our adventure with Imogen the Ice Dance Fairy," she confessed, still holding onto the rail around the rink.

"Didn't you say you'd been having ice-skating lessons back home in Wetherbury, Kirsty? You must be brilliant by now!"

Kirsty laughed. "Not really," she replied, skating back towards Rachel. "My coach has been teaching me some simple figure skating, that's all."

Rachel looked impressed. "I can't do *anything* like that," she said. "I can stay upright and skate around, and that's all!

Show me what you've been learning, Kirsty."

"OK, I'll do a simple figure-of-eight first," Kirsty explained. "When I've finished, you should see a perfect figure-of-eight drawn on the ice!" She struck out, leaning on the outside edge of her skate, but immediately she lost her balance and tumbled over.

"Ouch!" Kirsty gasped.

"Are you all right?" Rachel asked.

"Fine!" Kirsty called back, climbing quickly to her feet. "I fell over all the time while I was practising!"

Rachel watched as Kirsty tried again. This time she managed to complete one of the circles that made up the figure-of-eight. But when she leaned outwards on the opposite side to complete the move, her foot slipped and she went skidding across the ice.

"This isn't your fault, Kirsty," Rachel said sadly. "It's because Isla's magic star is missing!"

"And this is *exactly* what's going to happen when the auditions start," Kirsty agreed. "The skaters will be slipping and sliding everywhere *and* falling over. It'll be a disaster!"

Chaos in the Rink!

Rachel watched as Kirsty tried some more figure-skating moves. But however hard Kirsty concentrated, she just couldn't complete any of them properly.

Then the girls heard voices. The double doors at the side of the rink opened, and Rachel and Kirsty saw a boy and a girl dressed in glittering white skating costumes trimmed with gold fringes.

They were carrying
their matching
white and gold ice
skates over their
shoulders.

"It's Kayla and
Adam!" Rachel told
Kirsty, waving at them.

"Hi, Rachel," Adam said
with a grin. He and Kayla sat down and
swiftly pulled on their skates. "I'm really
glad you're here to support us."

"And this is my friend, Kirsty," Rachel
told them. "She's been coming to all the
auditions with me this week."

"Your outfits are *amazing!*" Kirsty
said, her eyes wide. Kayla and Adam's
costumes were covered in tiny sequins
that shimmered in the lights.

"Thanks." Kayla smiled at her. "The other skaters have gorgeous costumes, too!" She glanced at the double doors. They could hear more voices and footsteps. "Here they come now."

The doors were flung open again, and a whole crowd of skaters hurried into the rink. As Kayla had said, they were all dressed in stunning costumes in bright colours like scarlet, aquamarine and gold, and their outfits were trimmed with feathers, fringes, sequins, diamanté and ribbons.

Rachel and Kirsty stared closely at all the competitors, but none of them looked like goblins in disguise.

"Everyone wants to do well today," Kayla confided to Kirsty and Rachel as the other competitors began to pull on their skates. "The auditions are being judged by Dominic Grant and Helena Mitchell. Have you heard of them, Kirsty?"

"Oh, yes!" Kirsty said eagerly.

"They're champion figure skaters, aren't they? I've seen them on TV."

"Dominic and Helena are from Tippington," Kayla explained, "but they travel all around the world to skating competitions. They've won lots of medals!"

"And that's why everybody's so nervous," Adam added. "We all want to impress them!"

Kayla nudged Kirsty. "Here they come!" she whispered in an excited voice.

A tall dark-haired man and a slim blonde woman had just walked into the rink. They were each carrying a clipboard.

"Hello, everybody!" called Dominic Grant with a smile. "Welcome to the ice-skating audition for the Tippington Variety Show. I'll just check to make sure that everyone's present, so please call out *here* when I say your school's name."

Dominic began to read out the list of schools taking part, and everyone, including Adam and Kayla, obediently said *here*. But when Dominic mentioned 'Icy Towers', there was complete silence. Rachel and Kirsty frowned. "Icy Towers don't seem to be here," Dominic said to Helena, raising his eyebrows. "Maybe they're late."

"Well, if they don't arrive soon, they'll miss the audition," Helena Mitchell replied. "It'll be starting shortly." She turned to the skaters. "Why don't you use this time to warm up on the ice and practise your routine before the audience comes in?" she said.

Kirsty and Rachel glanced at each other in concern as Adam and Kayla skated onto the ice.

"We don't have much time to find the magic star!" Kirsty whispered to Rachel. "Where *are* the goblins?"

"I don't know," Rachel muttered. "But

we'd better get out of the way and let
everyone practise for the audition."

Quickly, the girls stood to one side
at the rail. As the skaters began their
routines, Rachel's eyes widened with
delight. All the skaters, including Adam
and Kayla, were performing spectacular
loops, lifts, jumps and
other complicated
moves.

"This is
amazing!"
Rachel gasped,
marvelling
at Adam and
Kayla's speed as
they flew around the
rink, travelling forwards *and* backwards.
"And look at those two, Kirsty!"

A couple dressed in midnight-blue costumes decorated with silver stars were both crouched down low and spinning around on the ice with one leg extended.

"That's a sit-spin," Kirsty explained.

Rachel glanced at Adam and Kayla again. Adam had just spun Kayla around, and now, holding hands, they were setting off on another fast tour of the rink. But suddenly, at exactly the same moment, they both tripped heavily.

"Oh!" Kayla gasped as she sprawled out on the ice. She didn't look hurt, Rachel and Kirsty were glad to see — just surprised.

"What went wrong? We're usually good at that move!" said Adam.

Before Adam and Kayla could get to their feet, the couple dressed in midnight-blue had also begun slipping and sliding around on the ice, and then they too tumbled over.

"Stop!" shrieked one of the other girls, trying to come to a halt as her partner whizzed her round.

"My laces have come undone!" She stumbled over her trailing laces and tripped, dragging her partner down with her.

Meanwhile, another boy tried to catch his partner as she jumped towards him, but he missed. With a gasp, she fell to the ice.

"Everything's going wrong!" Kirsty groaned as the girl climbed unsteadily to her feet. All the skaters' sharp blades were sending showers of ice flying up into the air as they struggled to keep their balance. "What are we going to do, Rachel?"

Rachel didn't reply. She was staring hard at a shower of ice that seemed to be lingering and sparkling in the air close by, just above the surface of the rink.

"Look, Kirsty!" Rachel whispered, her heart thumping with excitement. "I can see Isla the Ice Star Fairy!"

Goblins On Ice!

Kirsty gave a gasp of surprise as she also spotted Isla. A tiny hand waved at them. Then Isla zoomed past them in a dazzling blur and dived behind one of the rows of seats. Quickly the girls pulled off their skates and rushed to join her.

"Oh, Isla, we're so glad to see you!" Kirsty blurted out as Isla popped up to greet them. "The ice audition is going to be a *disaster*!"

"I know." Isla heaved a huge sigh. She was wearing an aqua-coloured all-in-one skating catsuit with a sheer, shimmery lilac skirt over the top, and matching ice skates. "We *must* get my magic star back from the goblins before the audition starts."

"But we don't even know where the goblins *are*," Rachel pointed out despairingly.

Isla smiled. "I do!" she told them. "They're in Fairyland at Jack Frost's Ice Castle, practising for the audition with my magic star! Will you go there with me, girls?"

"Of course we will!" Rachel and Kirsty cried.

Swiftly, Isla waved her wand and a
shower of magical fairy dust floated
down around the girls. They began
to shrink straightaway until, just a few
seconds later,
Rachel and
Kirsty were
the same size
as Isla, with
the same
translucent

fairy wings on their shoulders. Then
another flick of Isla's wand whisked the
three friends off to Fairyland!

When the glittering mist of fairy
dust cleared, Rachel and Kirsty found
themselves hiding behind the branch
of a frozen tree, just outside Jack Frost's
Ice Castle. The girls had visited the castle

several times before, but the sight of the
ice-blue towers and turrets against
the gloomy grey sky always sent
a shiver down their spines.

"Look!" Isla pointed
her wand at the
castle moat.
"There are the
goblins! I'd
better make us
extra-small so
that they don't
see us."

The castle moat was
frozen solid. The goblins
were whizzing round and round it,
showing off their ice-skating skills. They
all wore different sparkly costumes that
were just as colourful as the ones that

Adam, Kayla and the other skaters had been wearing. The goblins also had enormous ice skates on their big feet.

They were performing all sorts of amazing jumps, twirls and spins as they skated along.

Suddenly, Rachel spotted something that made her heart beat faster. "See that goblin in the gold trousers and pink shirt?" she whispered to Kirsty and Isla. "I think he has the star!"

Isla and Kirsty looked more closely at the goblin Rachel had spotted. He was skating along very fast and performing flips, loops and jumps at great speed.

In his hand was a golden star, and Kirsty could just make out a picture of an ice skate etched on its glittering surface.

"It *is* my star!" Isla exclaimed.

At that moment the goblin with the star did an elaborate twirl, spinning round and round and round until he was just a blur. Looking very annoyed, another goblin leaned over and grabbed the star from him.

"Hey, give that back!" the first goblin shouted furiously.

The second goblin ignored him and began gliding along on one leg with the other held out high up behind him.

"Look at me!" he shouted proudly. "If anyone's taking part in the Tippington ice-skating audition, it should be me. I'm the best!"

Then he gave a squeal of outrage as a bigger goblin snatched the star from him.

"No way!" proclaimed the bigger goblin, showing off an impressive sequence of spins and enormous jumps high into the air. "I'm a much better skater than you! Icy Towers are going to win the audition!"

The goblins cheered loudly, but then they started squabbling again as one of them sneaked up and pinched the star for himself.

He skated off swiftly with the others in hot pursuit.

"The goblins haven't made it to the audition yet because they're arguing about which two of them are going to take part!" Isla whispered to Rachel and Kirsty. "So we still have time to get the star back."

"But how?" Rachel wanted to know. "The goblins keep grabbing the star from each other, so it's going to be difficult to get the star away from them—"

"Not if *I'm* disguised as a goblin!"
Kirsty broke in.

Isla and Rachel stared at her.

"If Isla can make me look like a
goblin, then I'm a good enough skater
to keep up with them,"
Kirsty explained
quickly, as the
goblins whizzed
out of sight
around the
back of the
Ice Castle.
"I can get
in the middle
of them and
snatch the star!"

"Can you do that,
Isla?" asked Rachel eagerly.

Isla nodded. "But without the star, my magic is weaker than normal," she warned Kirsty as they all flew down from the tree. "The disguise might not last long, so you'll have to be quick."

"I'll do my best," Kirsty promised.

Isla twirled her wand and directed a stream of magical fairy sparkles at Kirsty. Instantly Kirsty became goblin-sized. The T-shirt and jeans that she was wearing vanished, and she was now dressed in a shimmering purple leotard and leggings, with a purple trilby hat hiding her hair, and silver skates on her feet. Kirsty glanced down at herself and grinned when she saw that her hands were green.

"Your nose is long, too, just like the goblins!" Rachel told her with a smile.

At that moment the goblins came racing around the side of the castle, still chasing the one who had Isla's star. Quickly, Kirsty joined the crowd of goblins and then she began to skate as fast as she could, weaving her way through the others towards the goblin with Isla's star at the front. Because the star was close by, Kirsty could skate almost as well as she usually could, and soon she was getting closer and closer to the front of the crowd.

"Let's help Kirsty by distracting the goblins," Isla suggested to Rachel. The two of them zipped over to the moat and then flew alongside the skating goblins, hovering just above them. One of the goblins spotted Isla and Rachel and gave a shriek of rage.

"Pesky fairies!" he yelled. "Don't let them get the star!"

All the goblins glanced up, giving Kirsty time to pass them all and draw almost level with the goblin who had the star.

"Look out!" Kirsty called in her best gruff goblin voice as Isla and Rachel swooped down again. "The fairies are going to steal the star from you! Give it to me for safekeeping!"

The goblin with the star hesitated. But then, as Kirsty skated alongside him, he held out the star to her. Breathing a sigh of relief, Kirsty reached out to take it.

But before she could do so, the Ice Castle drawbridge suddenly opened. It crashed down over the moat with a deafening *CLANG!*

"What's going on here?" roared Jack Frost furiously as he stomped out onto the drawbridge.

Skating Star

Kirsty's heart sank as all the goblins skidded to a halt. She'd been *so* close to getting the star back!

Jack Frost stood on the drawbridge, glaring. He wore ice-blue pyjamas with a bunny pattern on them and a nightcap with a tassel hanging off the end.

"You're disturbing my afternoon nap!" Jack Frost declared angrily. "And why are you wearing those ridiculous clothes?"

"We – er – we're practising for the ice-skating audition," one of the goblins mumbled sheepishly.

Enraged, Jack Frost stamped his foot. "Get off the ice – right now!" he ordered.

The goblins all climbed
onto the drawbridge,
balancing shakily
on the blades
of their skates.
Kirsty didn't
want to draw
attention to
herself so she
had no choice
but to follow them.
She glanced up and saw Isla and Rachel
hovering above the castle entrance
behind Jack Frost. They looked worried.

"You're supposed to be *ruining* the
auditions, not joining in!" Jack Frost
fumed as the goblins huddled together on
the drawbridge. "How dare you disobey
my orders?"

"But the auditions are fun," one of the goblins protested faintly.

"And we're brilliant skaters," another added. "We're sure to win!"

"Yes, we're the best!" said another, and there was a chorus of agreement.

"Silence!" Jack Frost thundered. He pointed his ice wand at the moat and let fly a magical lightning bolt. Instantly the frozen moat melted into water, and the goblins groaned in dismay.

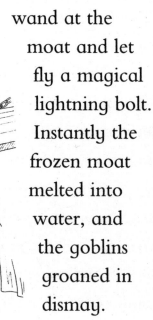

"I'll melt the ice at Tippington Ice Rink, too," Jack Frost said with smug satisfaction. "Then the audition will definitely be ruined!"

Kirsty was horrified. She looked up at Rachel and Isla once more, and could see that they were upset, too.

"But first I'll show you exactly who's the best skater!" Jack Frost went on. "Now, give me that star!"

Reluctantly the goblin handed it over. Jack Frost stalked back inside the Ice Castle and slammed the door behind him.

Grumbling, the goblins began to untie their skates, piling them up on a sledge that stood beside the moat.

"It's not fair!" one of them complained. "We could have been ice-skating stars!"

While the goblins were complaining, Kirsty seized the chance to slip away and hide behind the frozen tree again. Rachel and Isla fluttered over to join her.

"I was *so* close to getting the star back!" Kirsty sighed. "What are we going to do now?"

"You stay with the goblins and keep an eye on them, Kirsty, while Rachel and I see if we can find out what Jack Frost is doing with my star," Isla told her.

Kirsty nodded, then Rachel and Isla flew back towards the Ice Castle and began peeping in at all the windows to see if they could spot Jack Frost.

"There he is!" Rachel whispered, beckoning to Isla.

Jack Frost was rummaging in a wardrobe in one of the upper rooms. He was pulling out glittery outfits, one after the other, staring at them closely and then tossing them onto the floor. Finally he selected a sparkling blue costume, then he hurried into the adjoining room. Rachel and Isla flew to the next window and saw Jack Frost open a chest and take out a pair of ice-blue skates.

"What's he up to?" Rachel whispered to Isla as Jack Frost left the room.

Isla shook her head. "I have no idea!" she replied.

Although Rachel and Isla continued to fly around all the windows, they lost sight of Jack Frost for a little while. But at last they spotted a flash of blue heading downstairs again.

"It's Jack Frost – and he's changed his clothes!" Rachel murmured.

The door to the Ice Castle swung open and Jack Frost marched out onto the drawbridge. Kirsty and the goblins stared at him in surprise. Jack Frost was now wearing a glittery blue skating costume with icicles hanging from the collar, and he had a pair of skates slung over his shoulder.

"Follow me to the frozen lake," Jack Frost ordered the goblins as he strutted across the drawbridge, "And I'll show you the best ice skating you've ever seen!" He glanced at the goblins' sledge, now piled with skates.

"And bring that sledge with you," Jack
Frost added. "You can give me a ride
home afterwards!"

Grumbling under their breath,
the goblins dragged the sledge after
Jack Frost. Kirsty hung back a little,
wondering where Rachel and Isla were.
But then she heard
a voice close to
her ear.

"Rachel and I
are hiding in the
brim of your
hat, Kirsty!"
Isla whispered.
"Just stay with
the goblins and
don't let Jack Frost
out of your sight."

Jack Frost led the goblins to a frozen lake not far away from the castle. As the goblins gathered on the bank, Kirsty ducked down behind a rock, and Rachel and Isla fluttered off the brim of her hat to join her.

"And now prepare to be amazed!" Jack Frost shouted. He glided onto the ice and then skated around the lake, leaping and jumping and twirling and spinning, all at great speed and with perfect timing. The goblins' mouths fell open in shock.

"See?" Jack Frost yelled, as he went into a sit-spin so fast that he became an icy blur. "I told you I was the best!"

As Jack Frost skated backwards away from them, Rachel suddenly noticed something shiny hanging from his collar among the icicles.

"He's wearing the star!" Rachel gasped, pointing it out to Kirsty and Isla. "That's why he's so good!"

"But how do we get it back?" asked Kirsty as Jack Frost performed a somersault in mid-air, landing neatly on the ice.

Rachel smiled. "I have an idea!" she murmured. "Listen…"

Jumping Jack Frost!

The goblins were still watching in amazement as Jack Frost showed off even more. He was doing a series of twisting jumps, one after the other, when Kirsty glided out onto the ice in front of him.

"You're the best skater I've ever seen!" she exclaimed in her gruff goblin voice.

Jack Frost preened himself. "Yes, I am, aren't I?" he said proudly.

"Do you think you could show me a few moves?" Kirsty went on.

"Of course." Jack Frost grinned icily at her. "You'll never be as good as me, though!" And he grabbed Kirsty's hand and danced off across the ice with her. The next second they were flying across the lake at an amazing speed.

Kirsty gasped as they twisted and turned so fast that she was breathless after just a moment or two.

Jack Frost laughed. "Can't keep up, can you?" he jeered, skating even faster. He dragged Kirsty along with him, twirling her around until Kirsty's head was spinning.

The goblins were cheering and clapping so hard, they didn't notice Isla and Rachel hovering around the sledge piled with ice skates.

Rachel nodded at Isla, and the little fairy pointed her wand at the sledge and sent a stream of magic sparkles towards it. Immediately, all the skates rose into the air and floated noiselessly off the sledge. Another burst of fairy magic then sent the sledge sliding slowly across the ice.

Kirsty saw what was going on, and knew this was her cue. Gripping Jack Frost's hands tightly, she began to spin *him* round and round.

"We can go faster than *that*!" Jack Frost boasted, and together they spun around so quickly that Kirsty's hat fell off. Her hair tumbled down and at the same moment, Kirsty noticed with dismay that her hands were almost back to their normal colour. Isla's magic was wearing off!

Jack Frost let out an angry shriek.

"*You're* not a goblin!" he bellowed. "You're one of those meddling girls!"

"Let go NOW, Kirsty!" Rachel and Isla yelled together.

Quickly, Kirsty pulled her hands free from Jack Frost's. He wasn't expecting it and, unable to stop, he went spinning across the lake straight towards the sledge. Rachel and Isla were hovering there, hoping that the sledge would bring Jack Frost to an abrupt halt, and give them a chance to snatch the star from his collar. But as Jack Frost whizzed in the direction of the sledge, he spotted Isla and Rachel waiting.

"You'll never get the star away from me!" Jack Frost roared. As he approached the sledge, he crouched down and then sprang high up in the air,

zooming right over
the sledge, and
over Isla and
Rachel as well.
The goblins
cheered.

"*Wheee!*"
Jack Frost
crowed
triumphantly as he came down to land
on the other side of the sledge. "I told
you goblins I was the best!"

But as Jack Frost slammed heavily
onto the ice again, there was a loud
cracking noise. Rachel glanced down
and saw that the impact of Jack Frost's
landing had cracked the ice a little.
Immediately an idea popped into
Rachel's head!

I'll Be Back!

"Isla, can you make that crack wider?" Rachel asked as, grinning smugly, Jack Frost skated away from them.

Isla nodded. She pointed her wand at the crack and a shimmer of fairy magic swirled around it. Instantly the crack grew much bigger, opening out under Jack Frost's feet and revealing the water under the ice.

"Help!" Jack Frost yelled as the ice suddenly gave way beneath him. Then he plummeted into the water with a loud splash. Luckily, the water was only knee-deep, so Jack Frost quickly got back onto his feet.

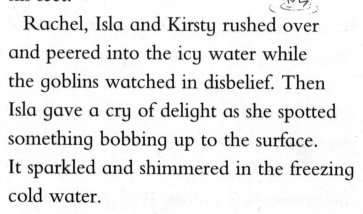

Rachel, Isla and Kirsty rushed over and peered into the icy water while the goblins watched in disbelief. Then Isla gave a cry of delight as she spotted something bobbing up to the surface. It sparkled and shimmered in the freezing cold water.

"Look!" Isla exclaimed. "It's my star!"

Quickly Isla fished her star out of
the water. The instant
she touched it, the
star shrank down to
Fairyland size, and
happily Isla fixed it
to the tip of her wand.

"Thank you, girls," Isla
said gratefully. "And now
we'd better help Jack Frost!"

Kirsty grabbed Jack Frost's arm as he
stepped out onto the ice. Jack Frost stood
there, dripping wet and glaring at them.

"You're drenched!" said Isla. "But
we'll soon fix that." She waved her
wand and a mist of fairy sparkles floated
down around Jack Frost, drying him off
immediately. But Jack Frost just scowled
even more.

"I'd better send you home straightaway, girls," Isla told them. "You'll be just in time for the start of the audition. It's lucky that no human time passes while you're in Fairyland! Nobody will have missed you."

As Isla pointed her wand at Rachel and Kirsty, Jack Frost stepped forward.

"You think you're so clever," he sneered. "But we still have the last

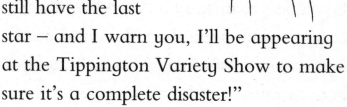

star – and I warn you, I'll be appearing at the Tippington Variety Show to make sure it's a complete disaster!"

As a cloud of fairy magic surrounded the girls and whisked them off home, Jack Frost's words were ringing in their ears.

"Do you think Jack Frost meant what he said?" Kirsty asked Rachel as they put on their skates later that evening. The audition was over 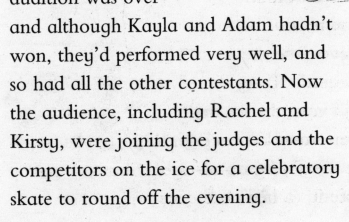 and although Kayla and Adam hadn't won, they'd performed very well, and so had all the other contestants. Now the audience, including Rachel and Kirsty, were joining the judges and the competitors on the ice for a celebratory skate to round off the evening.

Rachel nodded seriously. "Oh, yes," she replied. "He and the goblins are going to do their best to spoil the Tippington Variety Show. We *must* stop him!"

"So we'll have to get Taylor the Talent Show Fairy's star back before the show begins." Kirsty skated out onto the ice and performed a perfect move, leaving a figure-of-eight neatly etched on the ice.

"Come on, Rachel. You try it with me."
Rachel was still holding onto the rail, but bravely she let go, copying Kirsty's movements exactly.

"I did it!" Rachel exclaimed, staring down at the wobbly figure-of-eight she'd just drawn. "And I didn't even fall over."

"You're an ice star now, Rachel!" Kirsty laughed.

Now it's time for Kirsty and Rachel to help...

Taylor the Talent show Fairy

Here's an exclusive extract...

Flying the Flag

"Wow," said Kirsty Tate, as she walked into the Cooke football stadium. Music boomed out, and there seemed to be people everywhere, queuing for souvenirs, chatting to friends and heading to their seats. "It's buzzing in here!"

Her best friend Rachel Walker grinned at her, feeling excited. "It's the perfect place to spend our last night together."

Kirsty had been staying with Rachel for half term, and they'd come out this evening with Rachel's parents to watch the Tippington Variety Show, which was being held to raise funds for a nearby park. There was a large stage in the centre of the stadium, decorated with golden stars which glittered in the spotlights. The audience were dressed in different colours, according to which school they supported. Some wore green, some wore red, and some were in blue and gold, the colours of Rachel's school – Tippington School. Kirsty and Rachel both wore blue hooded tops and jeans, and had painted blue and gold stars on their faces.

"This is going to be brilliant," Rachel said happily. Then she frowned. "Well… if Jack Frost doesn't ruin it, of course," she muttered under her breath…

Read Taylor the Talent Show Fairy
to find out what adventures are in store for
Kirsty and Rachel!

Meet the Showtime Fairies

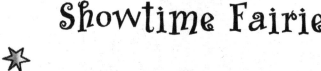

Collect them all to find out how Kirsty and Rachel help their magical friends to save the Tippington Variety Show!

www.rainbowmagicbooks.co.uk

Meet the fairies, play games
and get sneak peeks at
the latest books!

www.rainbowmagicbooks.co.uk

There's fairy fun for everyone on
our wonderful website.
You'll find great activities, competitions, stories and
fairy profiles, and also a special newsletter.

Get 30% off all Rainbow Magic books at

www.rainbowmagicbooks.co.uk

Enter the code RAINBOW at the checkout.
Offer ends 31 December 2013.

Offer valid in United Kingdom and Republic of Ireland only.

Nicki the Holiday Camp Fairy

Rachel and Kirsty have been looking forward to camp, but everything is going wrong. Can they help Nicki fix things, before the whole summer is ruined?

www.rainbowmagicbooks.co.uk

Meet the
Sweet Fairies

Lollie the Lollipop Fairy

Esme the Ice Cream Fairy

Coco the Cupcake Fairy

Clara the Chocolate Fairy

Madeleine the Cookie Fairy

Layla the Candyfloss Fairy

Nina the Birthday Cake Fairy

If Kirsty and Rachel don't find
the Sweet Fairies' magical charms,
Jack Frost will ruin all sweet treats for ever!

www.rainbowmagicbooks.co.uk

Alexandra the Royal Baby Fairy

Out in May 2013

Also available as an ebook

The whole of Fairyland is very excited - there's going to be a new royal baby! But when the special baby goes missing, Rachel and Kirsty are there to help their friend, Alexandra the Royal Baby Fairy.

www.rainbowmagicbooks.co.uk